WOULD YOU RATHER?

11 YEAR OLD
VERSION

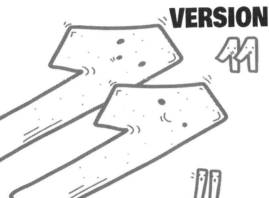

FOLLOW US AT:

f WWW.FACEBOOK.COM/ WOULDYOURATHERBOOK f

[O] @WOULDYOURATHERBOOK [O]

WWW.WOULDYOURATHERBOOK.COM

COME
JOIN OUR GROUP

GET A BONUS PDF PACKED WITH HILARIOUS JOKES, AND THINGS TO MAKE YOU SMILE!

GO TO:

https://bit.ly/3n9Nj5u

■ **Get a Bonus fun PDF** (filled with jokes, and fun would you rather questions)

■ **Get entered into our monthly competition to win a $100 Amazon gift card**

■ **Hear about our up and coming new books**

HOW TO PLAY?

You can play to win or play for fun, the choice is yours!

1. Player 1 asks player 2 to either choose questions **A** or **B**.

2. Then player 1 reads out the chosen questions.

3. Player 2 decides on an answer to their dilemma, and either memorize their answer or notes it down.

4. Player 1 has to guess player 2's answer. If they guess correctly they win a point, if not player 2 wins a point.

5. Take turns asking the questions, **the first to 7 points wins.**

(Note: It can be fun to do funny voices or make silly faces)

REMEMBER
Do **NOT** ATTEMPT TO DO ANY OF THE SCENARIOS IN THIS BOOK, THEY ARE ONLY MEANT FOR FUN!

WOULD YOU RATHER ?

11 YEAR OLD
VERSION

PLAYER 1

(ASK THE OTHER PLAYER(S) TO
CHOOSE QUESTION 1 OR QUESTION 2)

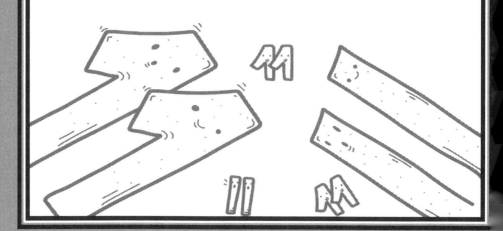

A — WOULD YOU RATHER

HAVE YOUR BIRTHDAY PARTY AT AN AMUSEMENT PARK

 OR

AT A ZOO?

B — WOULD YOU RATHER

ALWAYS BE THE BEST PLAYER ON A LOSING TEAM

 OR

ALWAYS BE THE WORST PLAYER ON A WINNING TEAM?

WOULD YOU RATHER ?
11 YEAR OLD
VERSION

PLAYER 2

(ASK THE OTHER PLAYER(S) TO
CHOOSE QUESTION 1 OR QUESTION 2)

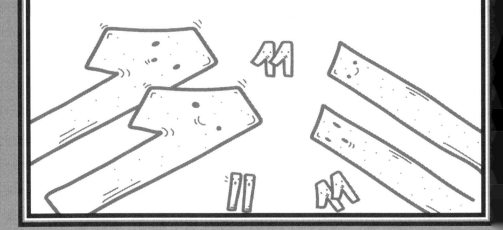

WOULD YOU RATHER

SPEND THE NIGHT IN PRISON

 OR

TRAPPED IN A COFFIN?

WOULD YOU RATHER

GO SNOWBOARDING

 OR

GO SURFING?

WOULD YOU RATHER ?

11 YEAR OLD
VERSION

PLAYER 1

(ASK THE OTHER PLAYER(S) TO
CHOOSE QUESTION 1 OR QUESTION 2)

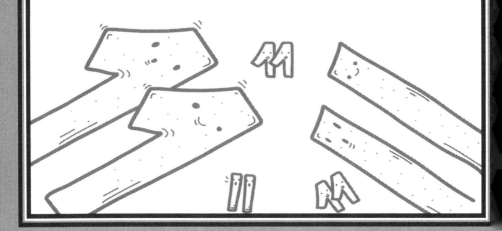

WOULD YOU RATHER

TALK BACKWARD FOR A DAY

 OR

WALK BACKWARD FOR A DAY?

WOULD YOU RATHER

BE OVERDRESSED AT A PARTY

 OR

UNDERDRESSED?

WOULD YOU RATHER?
11 YEAR OLD
VERSION

PLAYER 2

(ASK THE OTHER PLAYER(S) TO
CHOOSE QUESTION 1 OR QUESTION 2)

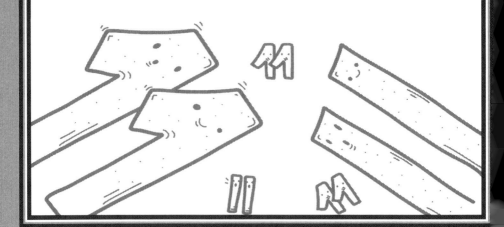

A WOULD YOU RATHER

HAVE THE LATEST PHONE

 OR

THE LATEST COMPUTER?

B WOULD YOU RATHER

TAKE PHOTOS

 OR

MAKE VIDEOS?

WOULD YOU RATHER ?
11 YEAR OLD
VERSION

PLAYER 1

(ASK THE OTHER PLAYER(S) TO
CHOOSE QUESTION 1 OR QUESTION 2)

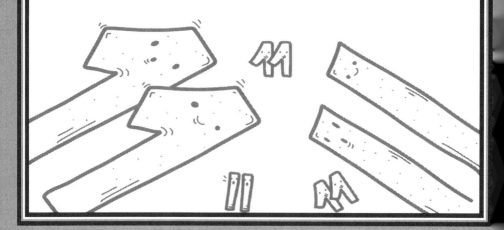

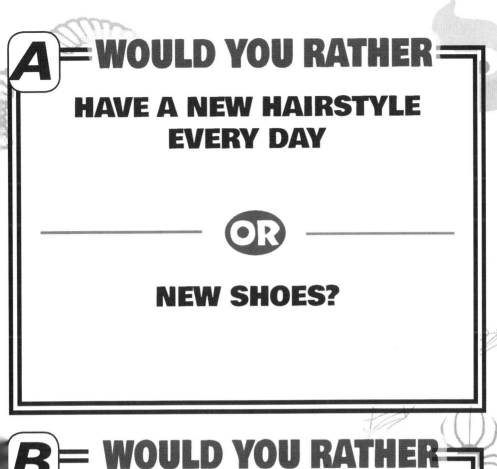

A | WOULD YOU RATHER

HAVE A NEW HAIRSTYLE EVERY DAY

OR

NEW SHOES?

B | WOULD YOU RATHER

VISIT EUROPE

OR

VISIT ASIA?

WOULD YOU RATHER ?
11 YEAR OLD
VERSION

PLAYER 2

(ASK THE OTHER PLAYER(S) TO
CHOOSE QUESTION 1 OR QUESTION 2)

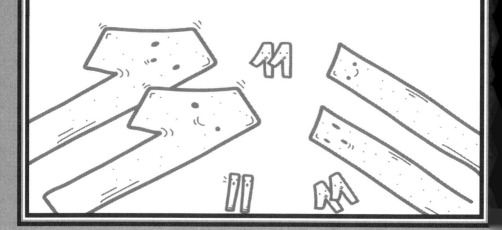

A WOULD YOU RATHER

ONLY EAT HEALTHY FOOD

 OR

ONLY EAT UNHEALTHY FOOD?

B WOULD YOU RATHER

BE KEPT IN A CAGE AT A ZOO

 OR

LIVE IN PRISON?

WOULD YOU RATHER ?
11 YEAR OLD
VERSION

PLAYER 1

(ASK THE OTHER PLAYER(S) TO
CHOOSE QUESTION 1 OR QUESTION 2)

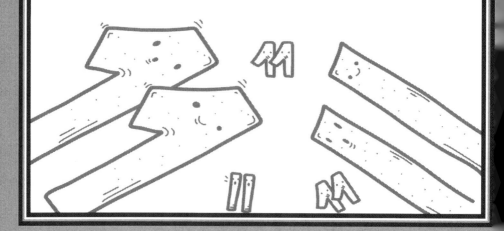

A = WOULD YOU RATHER

GIVE UP YOUR COMPUTER FOR A MONTH

 OR

NOT SEE YOUR FRIENDS FOR A MONTH?

B = WOULD YOU RATHER

WRITE A NOVEL

 OR

BE A JOURNALIST ?

WOULD YOU RATHER ?
11 YEAR OLD
VERSION

PLAYER 2

(ASK THE OTHER PLAYER(S) TO
CHOOSE QUESTION 1 OR QUESTION 2)

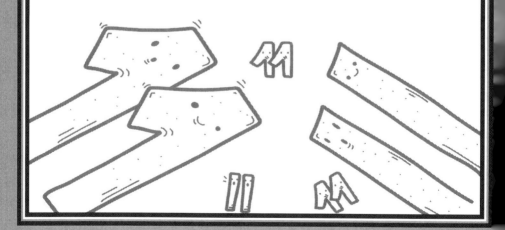

A — WOULD YOU RATHER

SAVE YOUR COUNTRY FROM A NATURAL DISASTER

 OR

A WAR?

B — WOULD YOU RATHER

BE THE TOUGHEST KID IN YOUR SCHOOL

 OR

THE SMARTEST?

WOULD YOU RATHER?
11 YEAR OLD
VERSION

PLAYER 1

(ASK THE OTHER PLAYER(S) TO
CHOOSE QUESTION 1 OR QUESTION 2)

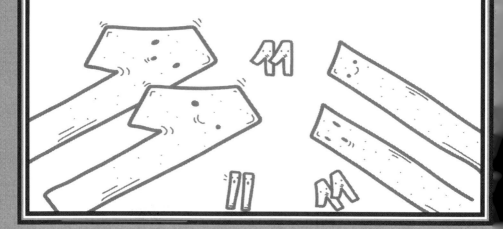

A | WOULD YOU RATHER

BE IN COLLEGE

 OR

BE IN HIGH SCHOOL?

B | WOULD YOU RATHER

BE A TOP FOOTBALL PLAYER

 OR

A PRO BASEBALL PLAYER?

WOULD YOU RATHER ?
11 YEAR OLD
VERSION

PLAYER 2

(ASK THE OTHER PLAYER(S) TO
CHOOSE QUESTION 1 OR QUESTION 2)

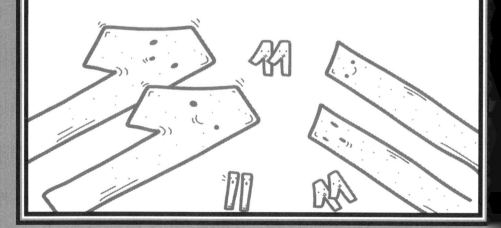

A WOULD YOU RATHER

BE IN A POP GROUP

A ROCK BAND?

B WOULD YOU RATHER

PAY SOMEONE TO DO YOUR HOMEWORK

GET PAID TO DO SOMEONE ELSE'S HOMEWORK?

WOULD YOU RATHER ?
11 YEAR OLD
VERSION

PLAYER 1

(ASK THE OTHER PLAYER(S) TO
CHOOSE QUESTION 1 OR QUESTION 2)

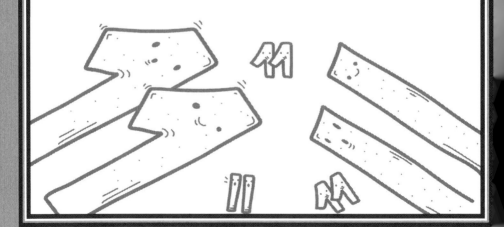

A — WOULD YOU RATHER

GET A GIFT EVERY WEEK BUT NO SAY OVER WHAT IT IS

 OR

ONLY GET GIFTS AT CHRISTMAS AND YOUR BIRTHDAY BUT GET TO ASK FOR WHAT YOU WANT?

B — WOULD YOU RATHER

END UP STUCK ON A DESERT ISLAND WITH YOUR MOM

 OR

YOUR DAD?

WOULD YOU RATHER?
11 YEAR OLD
VERSION

PLAYER 2

(ASK THE OTHER PLAYER(S) TO
CHOOSE QUESTION 1 OR QUESTION 2)

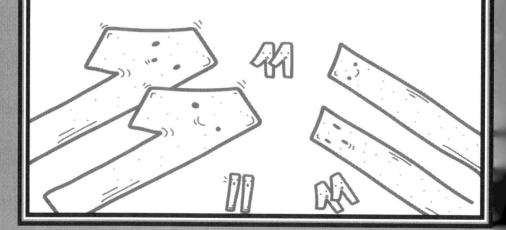

A — WOULD YOU RATHER

SAIL ON A YACHT

 OR

BE A PASSENGER ON A CRUISE SHIP?

B — WOULD YOU RATHER

HAVE REALLY TINY EYES

 OR

A MASSIVE NOSE?

WOULD YOU RATHER ?
11 YEAR OLD
VERSION

PLAYER 1

(ASK THE OTHER PLAYER(S) TO
CHOOSE QUESTION 1 OR QUESTION 2)

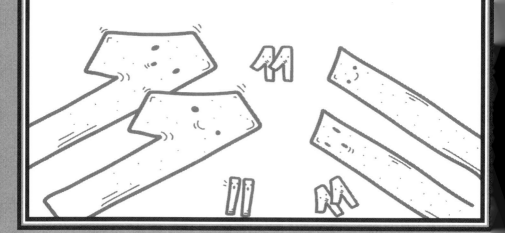

WOULD YOU RATHER

BE FAST AT TYPING

 OR

BE ABLE TO READ FAST?

WOULD YOU RATHER

SPEAK TOO QUICKLY

 OR

TOO SLOWLY?

WOULD YOU RATHER ?
11 YEAR OLD
VERSION

PLAYER 2

(ASK THE OTHER PLAYER(S) TO
CHOOSE QUESTION 1 OR QUESTION 2)

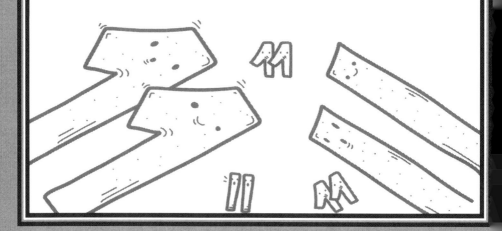

A | WOULD YOU RATHER

HAVE THE ABILITY TO CONTROL FIRE

 OR

CONTROL WATER?

B | WOULD YOU RATHER

BE DRIVING A SLOW CAR

 OR

BE A PASSENGER IN A VERY FAST CAR?

WOULD YOU RATHER ?
11 YEAR OLD
VERSION

PLAYER 1

(ASK THE OTHER PLAYER(S) TO
CHOOSE QUESTION 1 OR QUESTION 2)

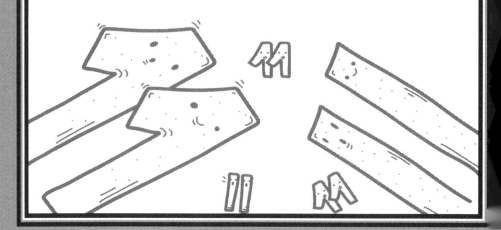

WOULD YOU RATHER

A

WATCH CARS IN A DEMOLITION DERBY

 OR

DRAG RACING?

WOULD YOU RATHER

B

BE BULLETPROOF

 OR

SURVIVE A FALL FROM A GREAT HEIGHT?

WOULD YOU RATHER?
11 YEAR OLD
VERSION

PLAYER 2

(ASK THE OTHER PLAYER(S) TO
CHOOSE QUESTION 1 OR QUESTION 2)

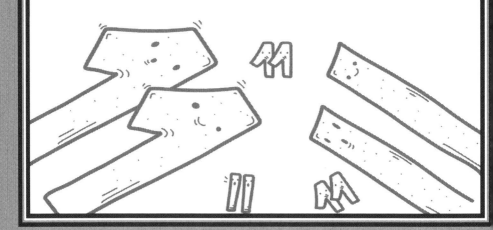

A WOULD YOU RATHER

NEVER HAVE GYM CLASS AGAIN

OR

NEVER BE ABLE TO PLAY SPORTS AGAIN?

B WOULD YOU RATHER

TALK ABOUT SCIENCE

OR

TALK ABOUT HISTORY?

WOULD YOU RATHER ?
11 YEAR OLD
VERSION

PLAYER 1

(ASK THE OTHER PLAYER(S) TO
CHOOSE QUESTION 1 OR QUESTION 2)

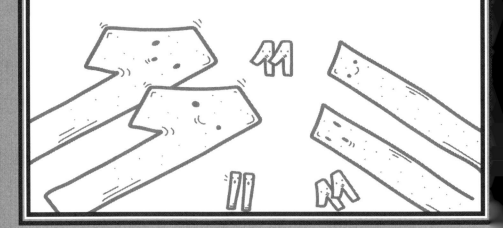

A WOULD YOU RATHER

ALWAYS WEAR SHORTS

OR

ALWAYS WEAR LONG TROUSERS?

B WOULD YOU RATHER

BE ABLE TO PUNCH THROUGH WALLS

OR

RUN THROUGH WALLS?

WOULD YOU RATHER ?
11 YEAR OLD
VERSION

PLAYER 2

(ASK THE OTHER PLAYER(S) TO
CHOOSE QUESTION 1 OR QUESTION 2)

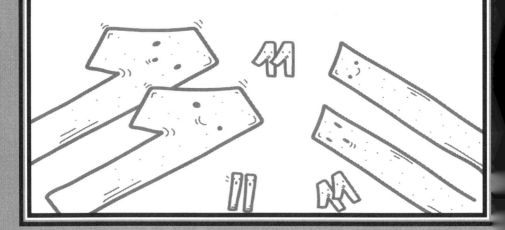

A — WOULD YOU RATHER

HAVE A HOLIDAY NAMED AFTER YOU

A PLANET NAMED AFTER YOU?

B — WOULD YOU RATHER

GO AND VISIT A NEW COUNTRY EVERY SUMMER

OR

BE GIVEN AN EXTRA MONTH FOR THE SUMMER HOLIDAYS?

WOULD YOU RATHER ?
11 YEAR OLD
VERSION

PLAYER 1

(ASK THE OTHER PLAYER(S) TO
CHOOSE QUESTION 1 OR QUESTION 2)

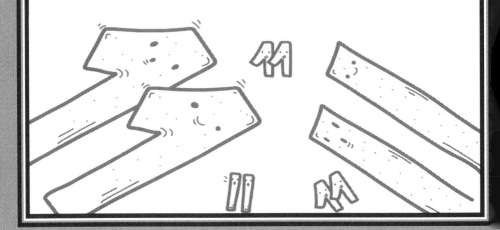

A WOULD YOU RATHER

GO ON SUMMER CAMP WITH YOUR FRIENDS

MEET NEW PEOPLE AT SUMMER CAMP?

B WOULD YOU RATHER

BE GIVEN THE ABILITY TO CHANGE YOUR SKIN COLOR

BE ABLE TO HOLD YOUR BREATH UNDERWATER FOR FIFTEEN MINUTES?

WOULD YOU RATHER?

11 YEAR OLD
VERSION

PLAYER 2

(ASK THE OTHER PLAYER(S) TO
CHOOSE QUESTION 1 OR QUESTION 2)

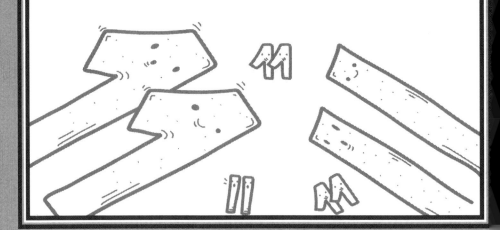

A WOULD YOU RATHER

LICK AN OLD STICKING PLASTER

 OR

LICK A BATHROOM FLOOR?

B WOULD YOU RATHER

HAVE ONE EYE

 OR

TWO MOUTHS?

WOULD YOU RATHER ?

11 YEAR OLD
VERSION

PLAYER 1

(ASK THE OTHER PLAYER(S) TO
CHOOSE QUESTION 1 OR QUESTION 2)

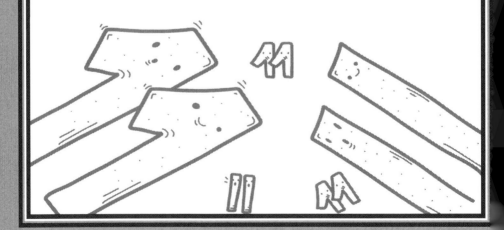

A WOULD YOU RATHER

EAT WHENEVER YOU WANT

 OR

GO TO BED WHENEVER YOU WANT?

B WOULD YOU RATHER

BE ABLE TO STAY OUT LATE AT NIGHT

 OR

HAVE A LIE IN EVERY MORNING?

WOULD YOU RATHER?
11 YEAR OLD
VERSION

PLAYER 2

(ASK THE OTHER PLAYER(S) TO
CHOOSE QUESTION 1 OR QUESTION 2)

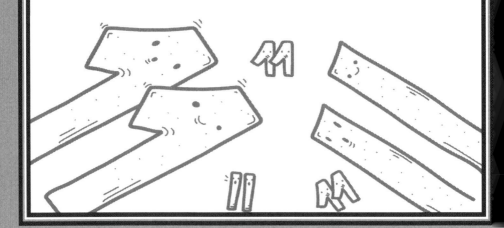

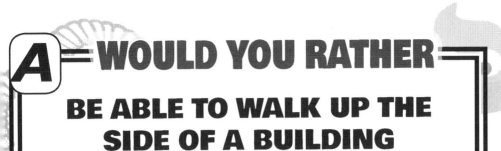

A WOULD YOU RATHER

BE ABLE TO WALK UP THE SIDE OF A BUILDING

OR

BE ABLE TO JUMP OVER A BUILDING?

B WOULD YOU RATHER

EAT AN APPLE CORE

OR

A BANANA PEEL?

WOULD YOU RATHER ?

11 YEAR OLD
VERSION

PLAYER 1

(ASK THE OTHER PLAYER(S) TO
CHOOSE QUESTION 1 OR QUESTION 2)

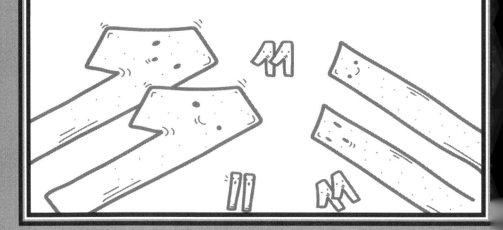

A | WOULD YOU RATHER

HAVE LONG TOENAILS

 OR

LONG FINGERNAILS?

B | WOULD YOU RATHER

ALL YOUR FINGERS WERE THUMBS

 OR

NOT HAVE ANY THUMBS?

WOULD YOU RATHER ?
11 YEAR OLD
VERSION

PLAYER 2

(ASK THE OTHER PLAYER(S) TO
CHOOSE QUESTION 1 OR QUESTION 2)

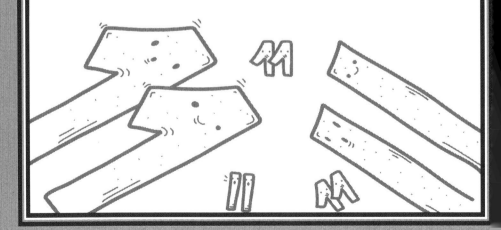

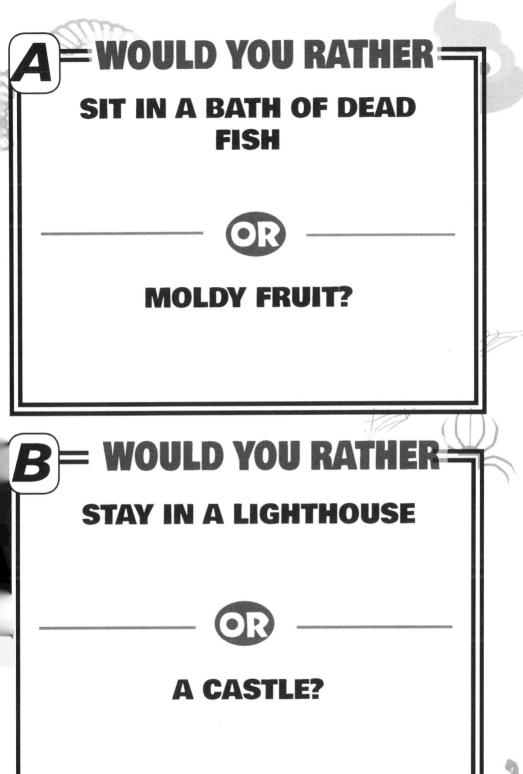

A = WOULD YOU RATHER

SIT IN A BATH OF DEAD FISH

OR

MOLDY FRUIT?

B = WOULD YOU RATHER

STAY IN A LIGHTHOUSE

OR

A CASTLE?

WOULD YOU RATHER ?
11 YEAR OLD
VERSION

PLAYER 1

(ASK THE OTHER PLAYER(S) TO
CHOOSE QUESTION 1 OR QUESTION 2)

A WOULD YOU RATHER

GUARD THE QUEEN

 OR

GUARD THE PRESIDENT?

B WOULD YOU RATHER

BE IN THE NAVY

 OR

THE AIR FORCE?

WOULD YOU RATHER?
11 YEAR OLD
VERSION

PLAYER 2

(ASK THE OTHER PLAYER(S) TO
CHOOSE QUESTION 1 OR QUESTION 2)

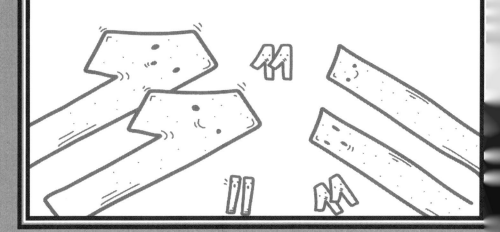

A WOULD YOU RATHER

NOT SHOWER FOR A WEEK

OR

NOT BRUSH YOUR TEETH FOR A WEEK?

B WOULD YOU RATHER

HAVE FASHIONABLE SHOES THAT ARE UNCOMFORTABLE

OR

WEAR COMFORTABLE SHOES THAT LOOK BAD?

WOULD YOU RATHER ?
11 YEAR OLD
VERSION

PLAYER 1

(ASK THE OTHER PLAYER(S) TO
CHOOSE QUESTION 1 OR QUESTION 2)

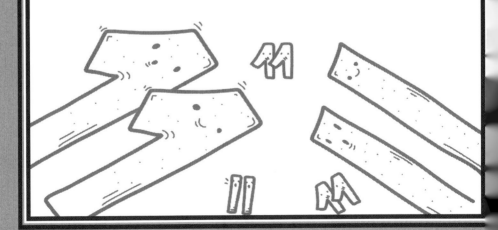

A — WOULD YOU RATHER

PLAY FOOTBALL WEARING A CATCHERS MITT

 OR

PLAY BASEBALL WEARING A FOOTBALL HELMET?

B — WOULD YOU RATHER

HAVE A MOTORBIKE

 OR

A CAR?

WOULD YOU RATHER ?

11 YEAR OLD
VERSION

PLAYER 2

(ASK THE OTHER PLAYER(S) TO
CHOOSE QUESTION 1 OR QUESTION 2)

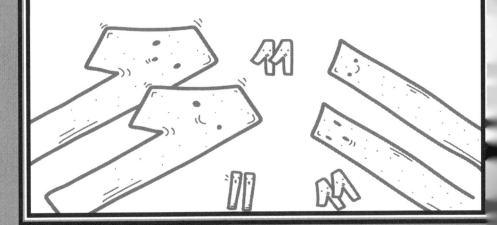

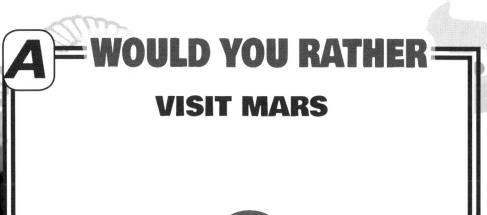

A | WOULD YOU RATHER

VISIT MARS

 OR

VENUS?

B | WOULD YOU RATHER

DRINK A GLASS OF COOKING OIL

 OR

EAT A JAR OF MAYO?

WOULD YOU RATHER ?
11 YEAR OLD
VERSION

PLAYER 1

(ASK THE OTHER PLAYER(S) TO
CHOOSE QUESTION 1 OR QUESTION 2)

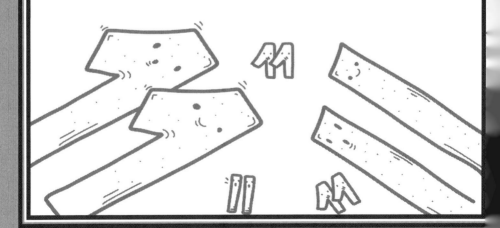

A — WOULD YOU RATHER

TRAVEL TWO HUNDRED MILES TO SEE YOUR FAVORITE BAND

OR

SEE AN UNKNOWN BAND IN YOUR TOWN?

B — WOULD YOU RATHER

LIVE IN A SMALL VILLAGE WHERE YOU KNEW EVERYONE

OR

A CITY WHERE YOU DIDN'T KNOW ANYONE?

WOULD YOU RATHER?
11 YEAR OLD
VERSION

PLAYER 2

(ASK THE OTHER PLAYER(S) TO
CHOOSE QUESTION 1 OR QUESTION 2)

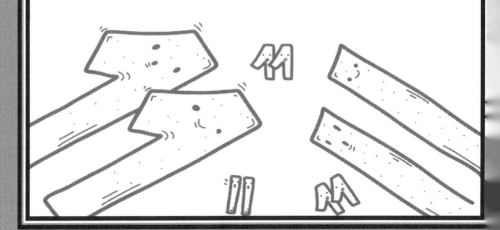

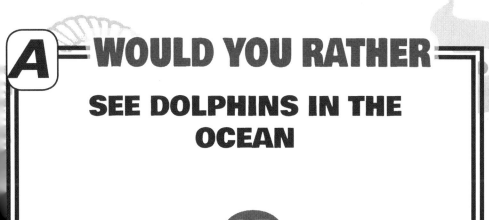

A — WOULD YOU RATHER

SEE DOLPHINS IN THE OCEAN

 OR

TURTLES?

B — WOULD YOU RATHER

BE LOST SOMEWHERE IN THE JUNGLE WITH A DOCTOR

 OR

A FIREFIGHTER?

WOULD YOU RATHER ?
11 YEAR OLD
VERSION

PLAYER 1

(ASK THE OTHER PLAYER(S) TO
CHOOSE QUESTION 1 OR QUESTION 2)

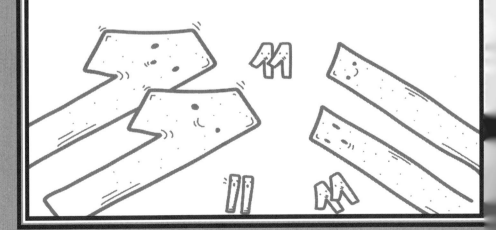

A WOULD YOU RATHER

HAVE TO LOOK AFTER A BABY

OR

TEN PUPPIES?

B WOULD YOU RATHER

LEARN TO WALK A TIGHTROPE

OR

LEARN TO JUGGLE?

WOULD YOU RATHER?
11 YEAR OLD
VERSION

PLAYER 2

(ASK THE OTHER PLAYER(S) TO
CHOOSE QUESTION 1 OR QUESTION 2)

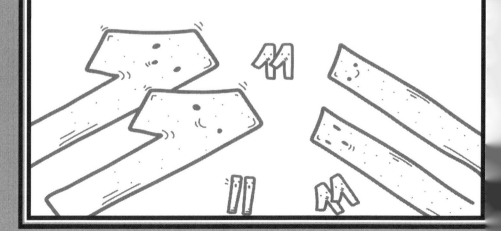

A = WOULD YOU RATHER

BE ABLE TO STAND AND DO A SOMERSAULT ON THE SPOT

OR

DO A BACKFLIP ON SKIS?

B = WOULD YOU RATHER

YOU HAD ONE LEG SHORTER THAN THE OTHER

OR

A HUMPBACK?

WOULD YOU RATHER ?
11 YEAR OLD
VERSION

PLAYER 1

(ASK THE OTHER PLAYER(S) TO
CHOOSE QUESTION 1 OR QUESTION 2)

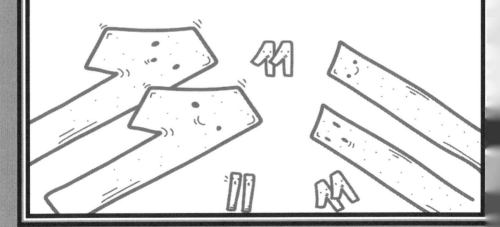

A WOULD YOU RATHER

BE LOST IN NEW YORK

 OR

YELLOWSTONE?

B WOULD YOU RATHER

YOU HAD A STAR NAMED AFTER YOU

 OR

A BEETLE?

WOULD YOU RATHER ?

11 YEAR OLD
VERSION

PLAYER 2

(ASK THE OTHER PLAYER(S) TO
CHOOSE QUESTION 1 OR QUESTION 2)

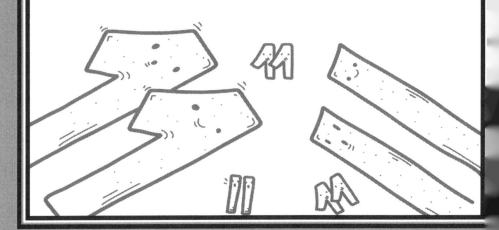

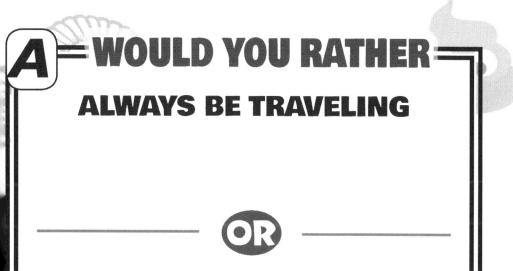

A WOULD YOU RATHER

ALWAYS BE TRAVELING

OR

BE RICH?

B WOULD YOU RATHER

HAVE A SERVANT

OR

A BODYGUARD?

WOULD YOU RATHER ?
11 YEAR OLD
VERSION

PLAYER 1

(ASK THE OTHER PLAYER(S) TO
CHOOSE QUESTION 1 OR QUESTION 2)

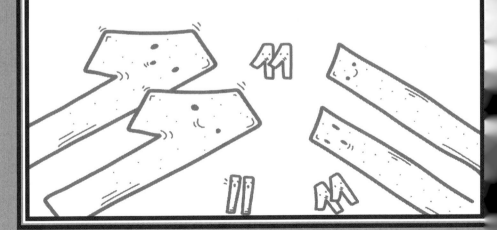

A WOULD YOU RATHER

HAVE TO WATCH A HORROR FILM

 OR

WATCH A COMEDY FILM?

B WOULD YOU RATHER

ALWAYS BE LATE

 OR

ALWAYS BE TOO EARLY?

WOULD YOU RATHER ?
11 YEAR OLD
VERSION

PLAYER 2

(ASK THE OTHER PLAYER(S) TO
CHOOSE QUESTION 1 OR QUESTION 2)

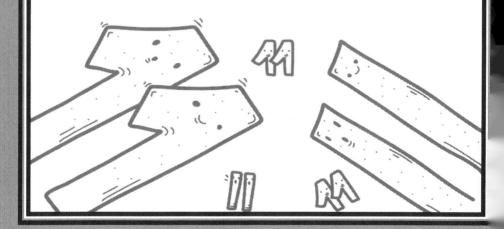

A = WOULD YOU RATHER

DRINK A TEASPOON OF CAR OIL

OR

A TEASPOON OF TOILET WATER?

B = WOULD YOU RATHER

NEVER CHANGE YOUR SOCKS

OR

NEVER CHANGE YOUR UNDERPANTS?

WOULD YOU RATHER ?
11 YEAR OLD
VERSION

PLAYER 1

(ASK THE OTHER PLAYER(S) TO
CHOOSE QUESTION 1 OR QUESTION 2)

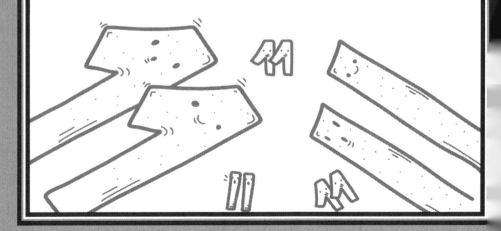

A — WOULD YOU RATHER

LOOK LIKE SOMEONE FAMOUS

 OR

BE FAMOUS BUT NO ONE RECOGNIZES YOU?

B — WOULD YOU RATHER

QUALIFY TO BE A LAWYER

 OR

A DOCTOR?

WOULD YOU RATHER ?
11 YEAR OLD
VERSION

PLAYER 2

(ASK THE OTHER PLAYER(S) TO
CHOOSE QUESTION 1 OR QUESTION 2)

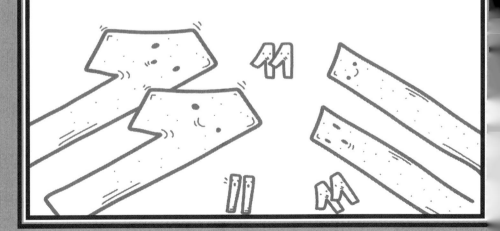

A = WOULD YOU RATHER

HAVE AIR CONDITIONING WHEN IT'S HOT

 OR

HEATING WHEN IT'S COLD?

B = WOULD YOU RATHER

LIVE IN CHAOS

 OR

BE BORED?

WOULD YOU RATHER ?
11 YEAR OLD
VERSION

PLAYER 1

(ASK THE OTHER PLAYER(S) TO
CHOOSE QUESTION 1 OR QUESTION 2)

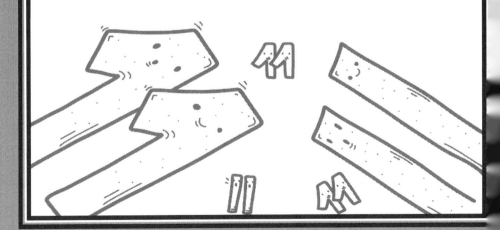

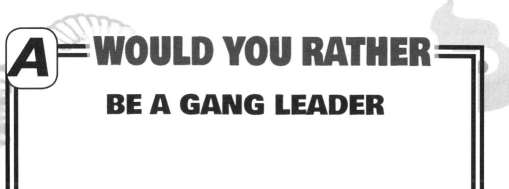

A WOULD YOU RATHER

BE A GANG LEADER

 OR

A VIGILANTE?

B WOULD YOU RATHER

LIVE IN A TRIBE IN AFRICA

 OR

IN THE AMAZON?

WOULD YOU RATHER ?

11 YEAR OLD
VERSION

PLAYER 2

(ASK THE OTHER PLAYER(S) TO
CHOOSE QUESTION 1 OR QUESTION 2)

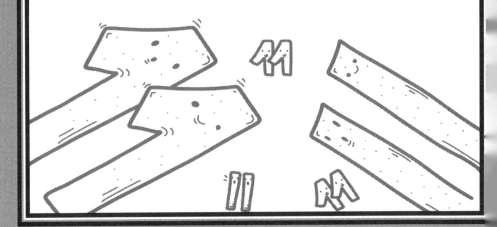

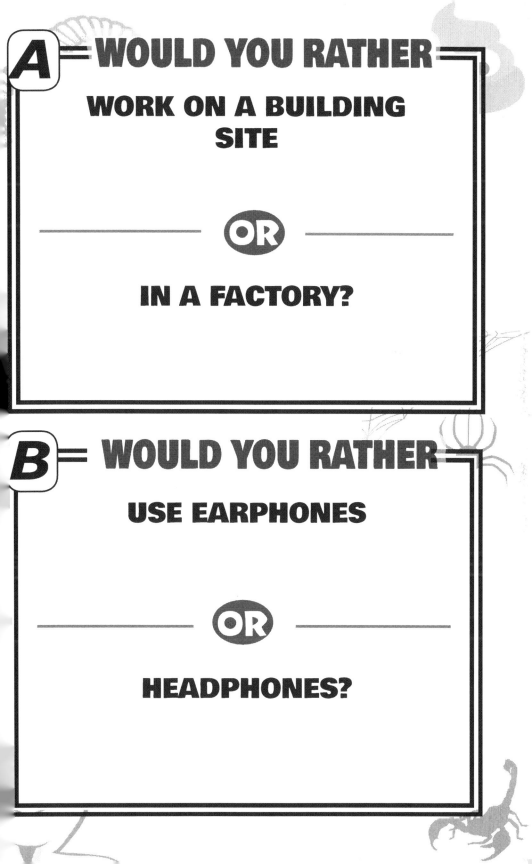

A **WOULD YOU RATHER**

WORK ON A BUILDING SITE

OR

IN A FACTORY?

B **WOULD YOU RATHER**

USE EARPHONES

OR

HEADPHONES?

WOULD YOU RATHER ?
11 YEAR OLD
VERSION

PLAYER 1

(ASK THE OTHER PLAYER(S) TO
CHOOSE QUESTION 1 OR QUESTION 2)

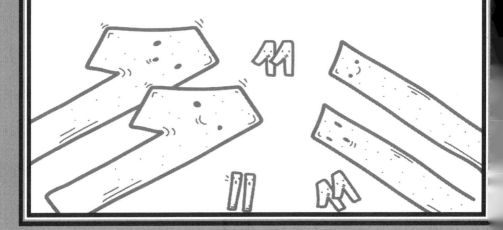

A — WOULD YOU RATHER

HAVE TO MAKE YOUR OWN CLOTHES

OR

CUT YOUR OWN HAIR?

B — WOULD YOU RATHER

HAVE NO PHONE

OR

NO INTERNET?

WOULD YOU RATHER ?
11 YEAR OLD
VERSION

PLAYER 2

(ASK THE OTHER PLAYER(S) TO
CHOOSE QUESTION 1 OR QUESTION 2)

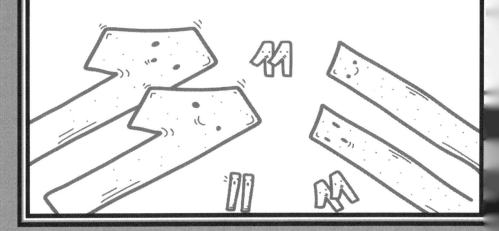

A WOULD YOU RATHER

BE STRANDED ON YOUR OWN

 OR

WITH SOMEONE WHO WON'T STOP TALKING?

B WOULD YOU RATHER

YOUR PARENTS CHOSE WHO YOU MARRY

 OR

BE SINGLE FOREVER?

WOULD YOU RATHER ?
11 YEAR OLD
VERSION

PLAYER 1

(ASK THE OTHER PLAYER(S) TO
CHOOSE QUESTION 1 OR QUESTION 2)

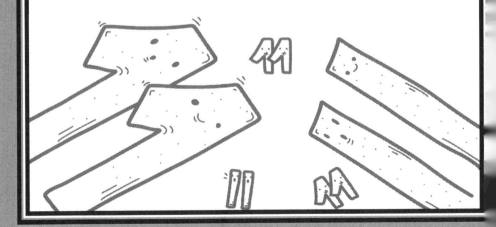

A WOULD YOU RATHER

HAVE GUARANTEED HEALTH

 OR

GUARANTEED WEALTH FOR THE REST OF YOUR LIFE?

B WOULD YOU RATHER

YOU ALWAYS HAD AN ITCH

 OR

WERE ALWAYS SNEEZING?

WOULD YOU RATHER ?
11 YEAR OLD
VERSION

PLAYER 2

(ASK THE OTHER PLAYER(S) TO
CHOOSE QUESTION 1 OR QUESTION 2)

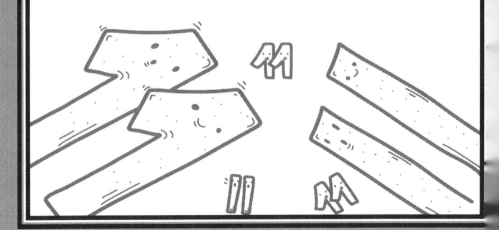

A = WOULD YOU RATHER

HAVE HAYFEVER ALL SUMMER

 OR

A COLD ALL WINTER?

B = WOULD YOU RATHER

LOSE TWO FRIENDS

 OR

GAIN ONE ENEMY?

WOULD YOU RATHER ?
11 YEAR OLD
VERSION

PLAYER 1

(ASK THE OTHER PLAYER(S) TO
CHOOSE QUESTION 1 OR QUESTION 2)

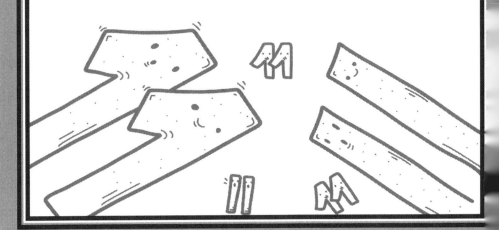

A WOULD YOU RATHER

BE A DOCTOR IN A PRISON HOSPITAL

OR

B WOULD YOU RATHER

HAVE A JETPACK

OR

GIANT ROBOT ARMOR?

WOULD YOU RATHER?
11 YEAR OLD
VERSION

PLAYER 2

(ASK THE OTHER PLAYER(S) TO
CHOOSE QUESTION 1 OR QUESTION 2)

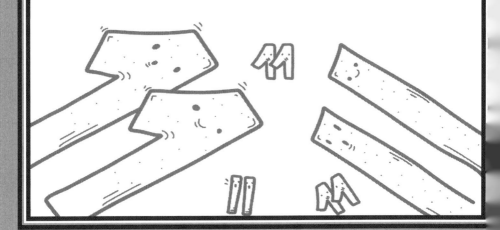

A | WOULD YOU RATHER

FEED ANIMALS AT A ZOO

OR

SEE ANIMALS ON SAFARI?

B | WOULD YOU RATHER

ALWAYS DRESS SMART

OR

ALWAYS DRESS CASUAL?

WOULD YOU RATHER ?
11 YEAR OLD
VERSION

PLAYER 1

(ASK THE OTHER PLAYER(S) TO
CHOOSE QUESTION 1 OR QUESTION 2)

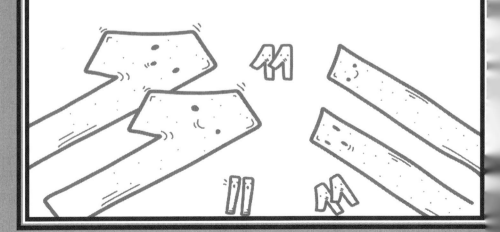

A WOULD YOU RATHER

STOP POVERTY

 OR

STOP CRIME?

B WOULD YOU RATHER

BE A STAR ON REALITY TV

 OR

MAKE A POPULAR YOUTUBE VIDEO?

WOULD YOU RATHER ?
11 YEAR OLD
VERSION

PLAYER 2

(ASK THE OTHER PLAYER(S) TO
CHOOSE QUESTION 1 OR QUESTION 2)

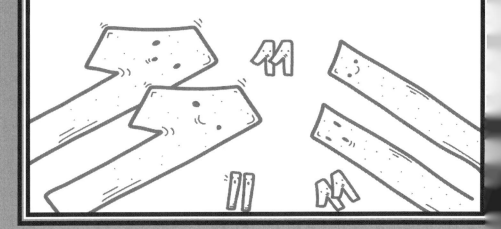

A = WOULD YOU RATHER

HAVE A FEAR OF ENCLOSED SPACES

 OR

A FEAR OF OPEN SPACES?

B = WOULD YOU RATHER

TRAVEL AROUND AMERICA IN A MOTOR HOME

 OR

TRAVEL ROUND THE WORLD ON A PLANE?

WOULD YOU RATHER?
11 YEAR OLD
VERSION

PLAYER 1

(ASK THE OTHER PLAYER(S) TO
CHOOSE QUESTION 1 OR QUESTION 2)

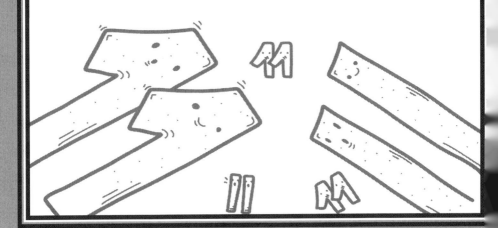

A | WOULD YOU RATHER

WAKE UP TO FIND YOU HAVE TWO HEADS

OR

FOUR ARMS?

B | WOULD YOU RATHER

BE SHOT FROM A CANON

OR

PUT YOUR HEAD IN A LION'S MOUTH?

WOULD YOU RATHER ?
11 YEAR OLD
VERSION

PLAYER 2

(ASK THE OTHER PLAYER(S) TO
CHOOSE QUESTION 1 OR QUESTION 2)

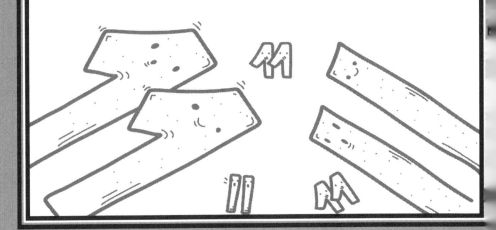

A — WOULD YOU RATHER

BE SUPERMAN

 OR

SPIDERMAN?

B — WOULD YOU RATHER

ALWAYS HAVE TO THROW UP ONCE A DAY

 OR

HAVE A HEADACHE EVERY DAY?

Made in the USA
Coppell, TX
08 January 2021

47750510R10057